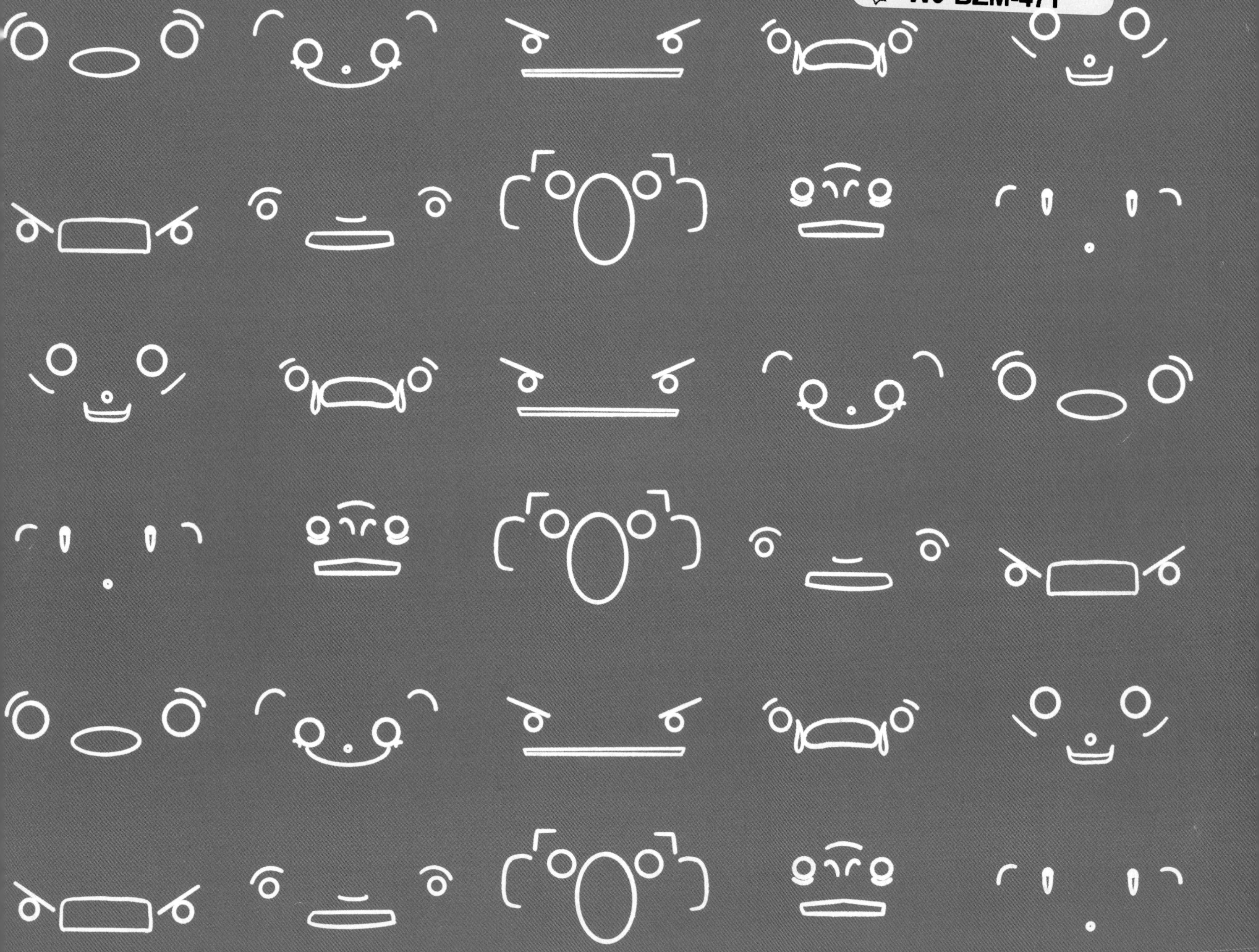

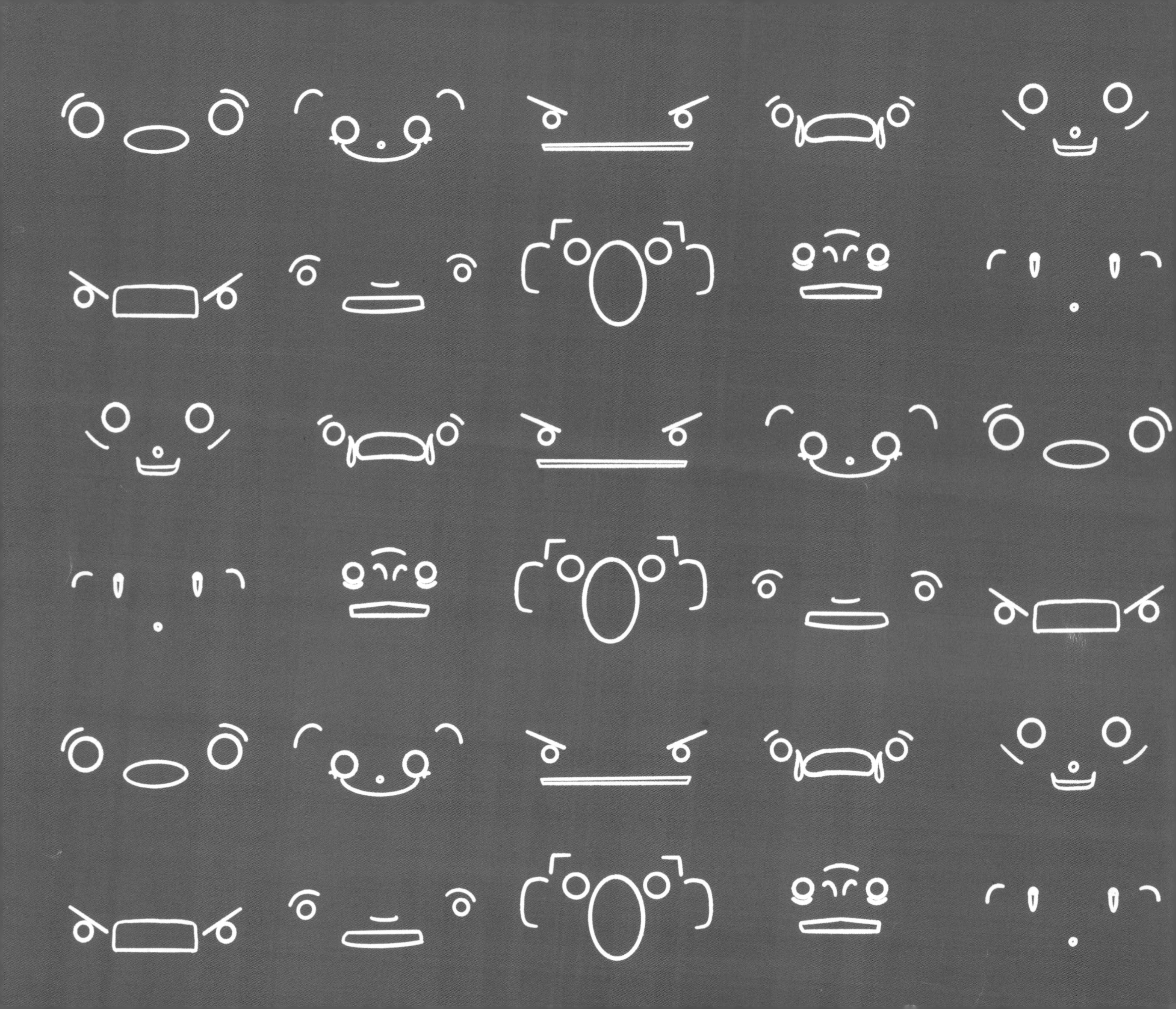

MOODY
MOODY
CARS

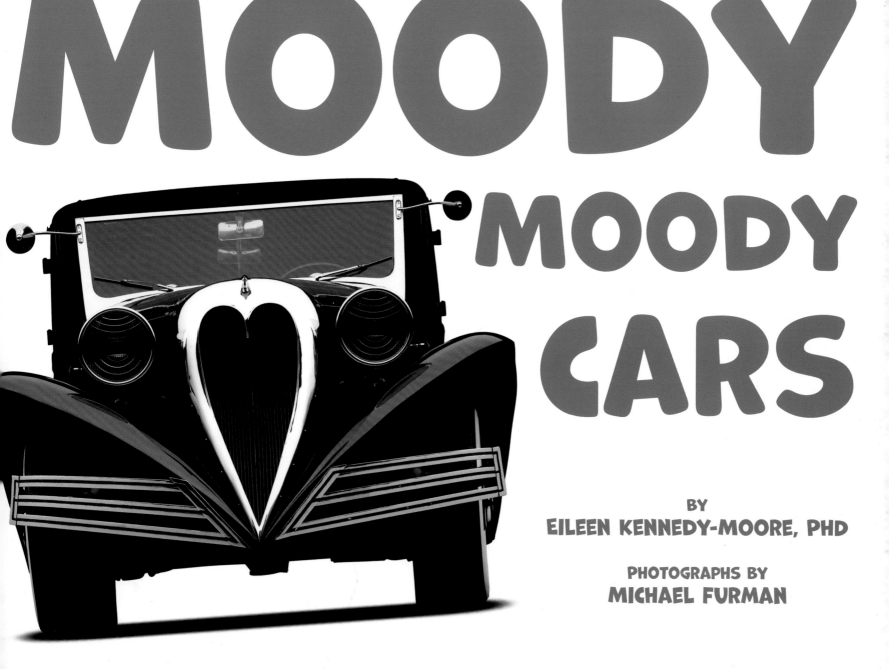

BY
EILEEN KENNEDY-MOORE, PHD

PHOTOGRAPHS BY
MICHAEL FURMAN

Magination Press · Washington, DC · American Psychological Association

For Mary, Daniel, Sheila, and Brenna, who
grew up spotting Moody Cars—EKM

For my wonderful children—MF

Books for Kids From the
American Psychological Association

Magination Press is a registered trademark of the American Psychological Association. Order books at maginationpress.org or call 1-800-374-2721.

Book design by Rachel Ross
Printed by Sonic Media Solutions, Inc., Medford, NY

Cataloging-in Publication data is on files at the Library of Congress.
ISBN: 9781433836992 (hardcover)
eISBN: 978143387005 (electronic)

Manufactured in the United States of America
10 9 8 7 6 5 4 3 2 1

HEY, MOODY CARS!
MOODY, MOODY,
MOODY CARS!
WATCHA DOING?
WATCHA SEEING?
CAN YOU TELL US
HOW YOU'RE FEELING?

"What's that?!" said a car
with wide-open eyes,
as it pulled to a stop,
with a look of

SURPRISE.

"I'm **AMAZED** and

ASTONISHED

at the thing that I see!
It's the circus come to visit!

GOT A TICKET FOR ME?"

Beep! Beep! went a car
with eyebrows pulled down.
"Hurry up! Running late!
See my traffic-jam frown?

I'm **MAD**, and
ANGRY, and
FRUSTRATED, too!

Slow-moving people need to

LET ME GET THROUGH!"

"Hello!" said a car
with a sweet little smile.
"Can you chat? Can you play?
We could visit awhile!
I am feeling very

FRIENDLY

with you here by my side.
I would like to get to know you,
so

LET'S GO FOR A RIDE!"

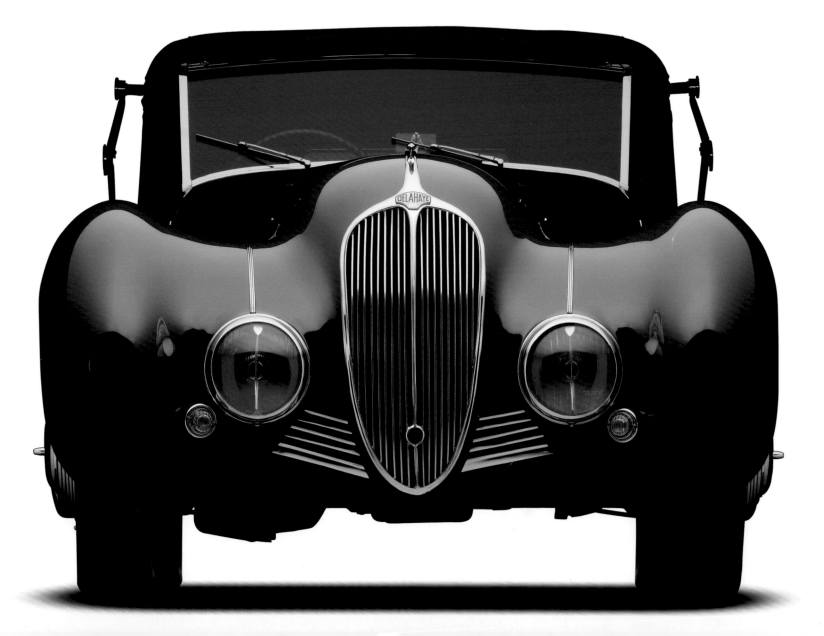

FREEWHEELING!

FULL OF FEELING!

TRAVELING NEAR AND FAR.

HONK IF YOU SEE ME.

I'M A MOODY MOODY CAR!

Winding through the
countryside, city, and town,
The roadways of emotion go
up and down.
You're swerving and a-curving
as you find your way.

HEY, MOODY CARS!

How ya feeling today?

"I'm **SAD!**" said a car with tears on its cheeks. "There's a sign where I park saying, *Closed for three weeks!* I was counting on relaxing in my favorite spot! I'm so

DISAPPOINTED!

"Va-room!" said a car.

"I feel **HAPPY** today!

What a **JOY** just to know

I can drive a long way.

I've got road beneath my tires.

I've got motor control.

My tank is full of gasoline;

I'M READY TO ROLL!"

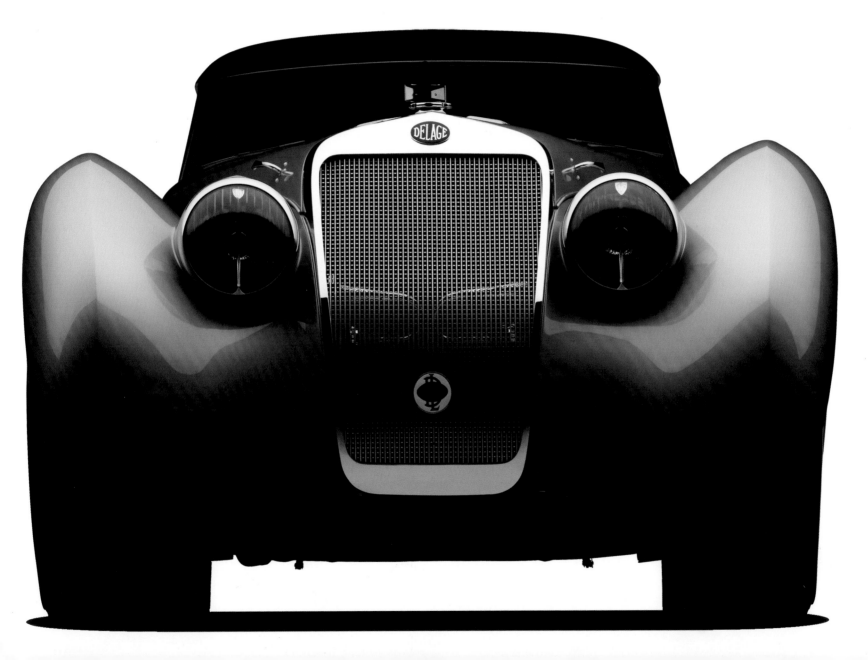

"Harumph!" said a car.
"I don't like this at all!
There's a new little coup
that's adorably small.

I'm so **JEALOUS!**

Filled with **ENVY**
of that little machine!
All this fussing for the
new ride turns my

RED PAINT GREEN!"

FREEWHEELING!

FULL OF FEELING!

TRAVELING NEAR AND FAR.

HONK IF YOU SEE ME.

I'M A MOODY MOODY CAR!

Emotions, like a compass,
guide your automobile.
They never last forever, but
they tell you how you feel.
Like seeing, touching, hearing,
they will show you your way.

HEY, MOODY CARS!

How ya feeling today?

"Oh, dear!" said a car, full of

WORRY and **FEAR.**

"I'm so **SCARED!**

Gravel road!
It could damage my rear.

I'm **AFRAID** that it will
scratch up all my beautiful
shine!

I'll just creep up very slowly,
guard this

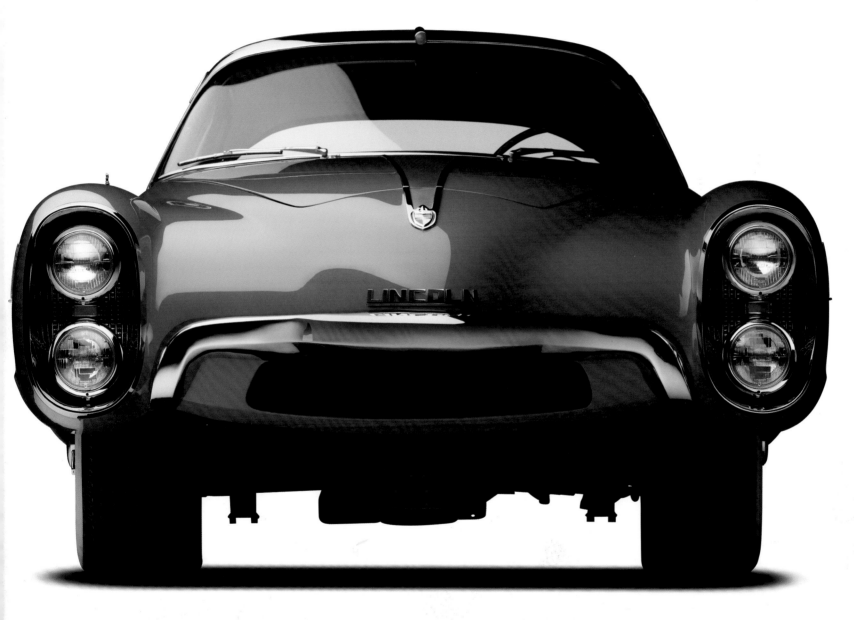

"Wa-hoo!" said a car,

with a shout of **DELIGHT**,
as it rolled, speeding down from

a **THRILLING** tall height.
"I'm **EXCITED** to be
driving on this big hilly road!

It's a roller coaster highway.

YEE-HAW! WATCH ME GO!"

"Pee-yew!" said a car,
tightly plugging its nose.
"Grab the soap! And some rags!
And let's turn on the hose!

I'm **DISGUSTED**

by the odor from that
smelly garbage truck.
He picked up all the trash;
now we can help him

CLEAN THE YUCK!"

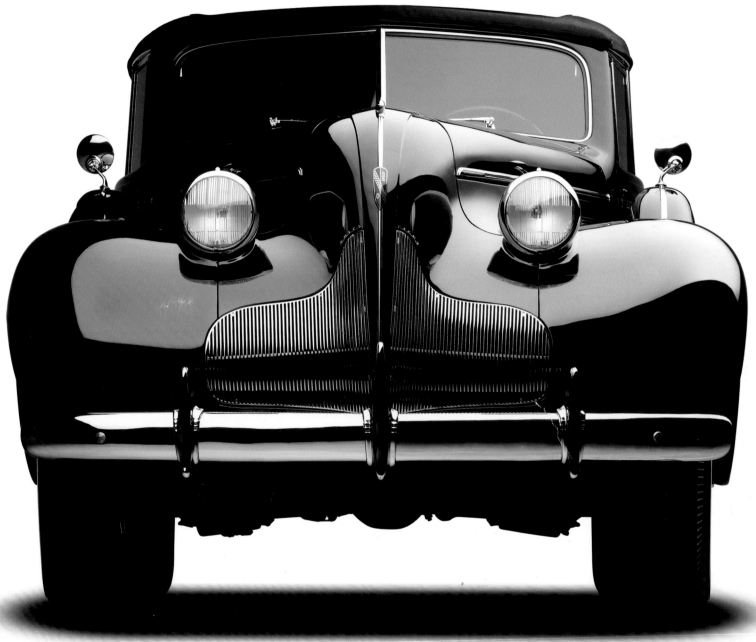

FREEWHEELING!

FULL OF FEELING!

TRAVELING **NEAR** AND FAR.

HONK IF YOU SEE ME.

Feelings and emotions,
they will come and go.
The more you understand them,
the more you'll know.
Talk and think about them, and
you'll find your right way.

HEY, MOODY CARS!

How ya feeling today?

"Shhh! I'm

TIRED,

and I'm trying to sleep!"

Oh.
Good night, Moody Cars.

SURPRISED

1956 Jaguar XK-D

FRIENDLY

1948 Delahaye

JEALOUS

1956 Buick Centurion

WORRIED

1955 Indianapolis

ANGRY

1959 Buick Electra Hardtop

SAD

1956 A.C. Cobra

HAPPY

1938 Delage Coupe

EXCITED

1938 Bugatti 57SC

DISGUSTED

1939 Buick Model 40

SLEEPY

1929 DuPont LeMans

READER'S NOTE

MOODY MOODY CARS is a playful approach to helping children learn about emotions. It's based on pareidolia, which is our tendency to see faces in things. Most children ages four years and up know that cars don't *really* have feelings, but it's entertaining and intriguing to see how these cars look as though they do! Figuring out the cars' expressions can help your child learn to recognize, label, and talk about these common emotions.

Understanding facial expressions of emotion is an essential skill that helps children navigate the social world. It allows children to know, for example, when a sibling is annoyed, or a parent sees danger, or a classmate wants to be friends. One study found that children's ability to interpret facial emotions at five years of age predicts how well they do socially and academically—even *four years later*. Research also shows that talking about feelings and practicing labeling them can help children increase their understanding of emotions. So, look for opportunities to talk about emotions in books, movies, and daily life.

Eye-tracking studies show that babies are very interested in faces—they'll stare at two dots and a curve arranged like a face longer than any other arrangement—but it takes children a surprisingly long time to develop the ability to recognize specific emotions:

- At two years old, children are only able to categorize photos of emotional faces as either happy or not. They tend to label all non-happy faces as angry.
- Around age three, children learn to recognize sad faces.
- Around age four, they can accurately categorize angry faces and distinguish these from other negative emotions. Being able to recognize fear, surprise, and disgust comes even later.
- Children show marked improvement in their accuracy at labeling facial expressions between ages five and seven, and their speed of labeling emotions and their ability to identify less intense emotions improves noticeably between ages seven and ten.

Learning to understand emotions may be especially important for boys. Too often, boys (and men) somehow get the message that emotions are "girly" and therefore not for them. But boys have feelings, too! As infants, boys are actually more expressive than girls, but by five or six years old, boys are less likely than girls to express hurt or distress.

Moody Moody Cars is a fun way to help all children develop emotional literacy, which is the ability to read feelings in ourselves and others.